Jack and Jill's Treehouse

Pamela Duncan Edwards

Illustrated by Henry Cole

KATHERINE TEGEN BOOKS
An Imprint of HarperCollins Publishers

For my Jack—Jackson Edwards,
because we have so much fun
playing together in his treehouse
—Love, Grandma

This is the branch
that held the treehouse
that Jack and Jill built.

This is the wood

that was hauled up to the branch

that held the treehouse
that Jack and Jill built.

This is the floor

that was made from the wood

that was hauled up to the branch

that held the treehouse
that Jack and Jill built.

This is the roof

that was raised over the floor

that was made from the wood

that was hauled up to the branch

that held the treehouse
that Jack and Jill built.

This is the light

that hung from the roof

that was raised over the floor

that was made from the wood

that was hauled up to the branch

that held the treehouse
that Jack and Jill built.

This is the table

that sat under the light

that hung from the roof

that was raised over the floor

that was made from the wood

that was hauled up to the branch

that held the treehouse
that Jack and Jill built.

These are the treats

that were piled high on the table

that sat under the light

that hung from the roof

that was raised over the floor

that was made from the wood

that was hauled up to the branch

that held the treehouse
that Jack and Jill built.

These are the friends

who gobbled the treats

that were piled high on the table

that sat under the light

that hung from the roof

that was raised over the floor

that was made from the wood

that was hauled up to the branch

that held the treehouse
that Jack and Jill built.

These are the birds who sang ``Good Night''

to the friends

who gobbled the treats

that were piled high on the table

that sat under the light

that hung from the roof

that was raised over the floor

that was made from the wood

that was hauled up to the branch

that held the treehouse
that Jack and Jill built.

HOORAY

for the treehouse that
Jack and Jill built!

Library of Congress Cataloging-in-Publication Data
Edwards, Pamela Duncan.
    Jack and Jill's treehouse / Pamela Duncan Edwards ; illustrated by Henry Cole.— 1st ed.
        p.   cm.
    Summary: A cumulative tale about Jack and Jill, who build a treehouse.
    ISBN 978-0-06-009077-7 (trade) — ISBN 978-0-06-009078-4 (lib. bdg.)
    [1. Tree houses—Fiction. 2. Building—Fiction. 3. Forest animals—Fiction.] I. Cole, Henry, date, ill.
II. Title.
PZ7.E26365Jac 2008   2006022241
[E]—dc22   CIP
                                                                                                                        AC

Typography by Carla Weise
1 2 3 4 5 6 7 8 9 10
❖
First Edition

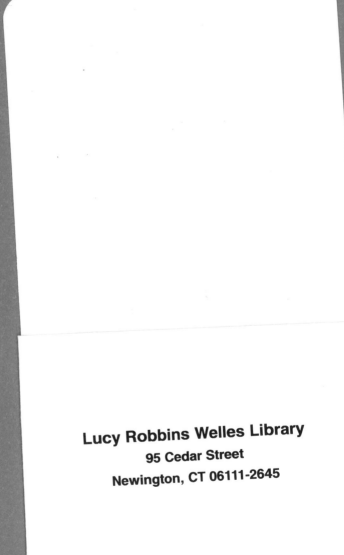